Rain and Eternity

By T.M. Craig

PublishAmerica
Baltimore

First printing

At the specific preference of the author, PublishAmerica allowed this work to remain exactly as the author intended, verbatim, without editorial input.

ISBN: 1-4241-0906-X
PUBLISHED BY PUBLISHAMERICA, LLLP
www.publishamerica.com
Baltimore

Printed in the United States of America

I would like to dedicate this book to the following people:

My Grandmother, My parents for their love and support. All of my close and dear friends who have read almost every story I have written and to those who were my inspirations: Amanda, Erin, Ashley M., Ashley W., Brittani, Natalie, Heather, and Bethany I love all of you and thank you for your support. My brother Punky and my sister-in-law Lynette for all the help and the little vacations. All of my teachers who have inspired me to be better, Mrs. Fox (not is not a verb no matter how hard you try and make that paper bleed because it can always be better), Mrs. Zoldowski (thank you for your advice), Mr. Simon, Mrs. Cox (a dear sweet woman who is very inspirational and loving), and finally Mrs. Noll (my favorite librarian who helped me whenever I needed it.) Thank you all for your love and support all through the years.

Part One

Prologue

Darkness surrounded him, engulfing him in a wave of sorrow; an untouchable force bounded him to this fate. He was doomed to walk the earth without love and very little hope for humanity remained in his ancient mind. The mountains were his only hope and only love. Many nights he has stared at the sky and bargained with the stars to help him rid himself of his wretched curse.

Gravel crunched under his black and white converse tennis shoes; his long blond hair fluttered as the wind blew through its thick strands. A small creek babbled beside him, he stooped to take a refreshing drink. His white cotton tee shirt glowed brightly in the still night. He appeared youthful and full of life, but his mind and heart was as old as the sky and as withered as the falling petals of a dead rose.

It has been over a hundred years since he made his deal with the she-devil. All he wanted to do was find love and live happily, but what did he get in return? He had to suffer through eternity without love and any feeling, but the deep undying hatred that consumed him entirely. Immortality in silence, breathing cold air and suffocating himself with his own dark and menacing thoughts; he was damned to walk this earth until the final minute of its own destruction.

He looked up from the creek; his green eyes smoldered like burning ambers. His mouth curled into a twisted glare as he stared into the sky. He picked up his worn suitcase and headed down the forgotten road that led into the heart of the mountains.

The sun followed behind him casting a shadow behind him as if it did not dare to cross his path. He could feel the rain falling from the angry sky as he walked down the deserted road back to the cold and bitterness that dwelled in his heart.

Chapter One
Lucy

"Come on Lucky let's go. We can not wait all day for you to get ready." Lucy's dad called impatiently to her. She finished packing the last of her things in a black backpack. She took one last look at her room. Her *old* room; the bare walls were white with black trim and her carpet was a faded blue. Everything appeared empty, hollow and somehow surreal. She walked out of the room and closed the door softly behind her. She exhaled deeply as she slowly walked down the stairs; her fingers glided across the worn banister inhaling the last of its comforting memories that it held beneath the wood.

"Come on Lucky we have to go. If we don't we will not get there before dark." Lucy's family was moving from Michigan to Kentucky because of what her father said was a new "job offer," but she knows it has to do with her mother's death. She knew her father needed a change of scenery, but she hated leaving her friends and her life behind.

"Everyone ready?" Her dad asked as he adjusted the rear view mirror to look back at her and her twin brother Johnathan.

"Yeah," Johnathan mumbled. He pulled his dark sunglasses from the top of his head over his eyes and crossed his arms. She could not see his eyes but she knew what he was thinking, *I wish I was never born.*

"Listen John, I do not like moving either but this a good opportunity for me and you guys. You have to deal with it like I am." Her father cautiously backed out of the driveway and drove to the busy highway. She stared out the window muttering good-byes to all the things she had come to know and love in her little town.

Johnathan sat next to her in their mini van with his player cranked all the way up and bobbing his head to the loud beat of a drum, trying to drown out the pestering clamor of the world. Her brother looked more like their father. They both had light mousy brown hair and misty gray eyes with tiny flakes of gold. Johnathan was as stubborn as her father was, but he kept to himself while her father loved socialize. He had loved going to parties with mother and hanging out with his friends at the club. Johnathan could sit alone in his room for hours practicing with his drums or talking to his friends online.

She, on the other hand, longed to be more like her mother Lilliana, with her long elegant auburn curls and laughing gray eyes. She had not only been lovely on the outside, but she was beautiful where it was most important, the inside. Lucy's long black hair never curled and her dark blue eyes were always clouded and full of thought. Her mother always said to her when she was little, "You are the mystifying one my little dark angel." Then she would sigh and hold her hand and whisper, "The mysterious one waiting for a grand adventure." Her mother would kiss her good night and leave to go to some wonderful party full of laughing people and long conversations.

"I am not like you dad." Johnathan whispered as he leaned back and stared at the tan roof of the van mouthing the words of every song that he heard. His arms were crossed against his chest.

Her father sighed and gazed at the road, tears clung to the sides of his eyes. "I am sorry." He choked back the tears as he turned left into the middle lane. His knuckles turned white from gripping the steering wheel tightly as he drove.

Lucy watched the scenery change from buildings with blinding lights and gas stations to mountains with pockets of bushy trees and rockslide signs. Traffic started to thin as they drove deeper and deeper into the reclusive mountains. "Finally a rest stop," her dad said sleepily. He was not use to driving, because his wife did all of the driving.

He quickly turned into the empty parking lot and stretched as he climbed out of the mini van. "Are you guys hungry? There is a vending machine down the hall and I could grab you something if you like." He yawned loudly as he rubbed his temple sleepily. .

She glanced at her brother, who had fallen asleep and his batteries in his player were running on low. She crawled over to her sleeping sibling and turned off his CD player and pulled a coat over him. He clutched the cover and curled into a ball near the window. Lucy stared out the window and looked to the sky, it was dark and the stars were the brightest that she has ever seen in years. She felt a wave of awe and a sense of freedom wash over her as she stared into the dark sky. She smiled as she prayed. *Mom, if you are there, please let everything work out. Please watch over daddy and Johnathan for when I cannot. I love you mom.*

She waited for her father for over twenty minutes before she quietly climbed out of the mini van and walked to the rest stop to find her father. She found him collapsed by a brightly-lit vending machine holding onto a bag of chips.

"Oh daddy," she whispered sympathetically as shook him awake.

"What? What? What?" He mumbled as his eyes fluttered open. "Oh, it is you Lucky. I must have taken a snooze." He staggered to the van and slowly sat behind the wheel. His tan arms hung limply at his side as he admitted defeat to fatigue.

"I am sorry Lucky I can not drive any more. I am worn out. I can barely keep my eyes open." Her father yawned as he rested his forehead against the steering wheel.

"Dad it is all right, I will drive. Remember I had got my license last week and I do know where we are going." She kissed the top of her father's head as he fell asleep in the passenger seat. Lucy sighed as she drove down the empty highway.

Her father tossed and turned as he slept. "I am sorry. So sorry," he repeated over and over again. He rested his head against the window and wrapped his arms around himself.

She turned on the radio and the soft melody hummed in her ears as she pulled into the deserted highway. Rain pounded on the windows as her father snored next to her and her brother twitched in the back seat. After and hour she slowly pulled into the driveway of her new home.

"Daddy we are here, time to wake up." He stirred and rubbed his eyes as he sat up. "Johnathan we are here." He ran his fingers through his hair and opened his eyes.

"When did it start raining?" Her father asked as he fumbled with his keys.

"Awhile ago after you fell asleep." She pulled her keys from her purse and flashed them in front of her father he smiled weakly and took them.

"I am sorry that I had fallen asleep Lucky." He yawned as he opened the door. Boxes were piled neatly in the living room and the furniture was neatly arranged in the dining hall.

"Daddy this place is beautiful. It is so large." Lucy whispered as she entered the massive living room.

"Yeah it is, isn't? Your mother grew up here. Your room is on the second floor, which is-I will let you explore tomorrow." He smiled. "Your bed should be up there and you need your rest. Johnathan your room is directly across from your sister's. Good night, I will see you in the morning." He yawned loudly as he headed up the stairs.

"Good night Daddy!" Lucy called to him as she elbowed her brother to do the same.

"What? I am not saying good night to him! Why should I? He moved us out in the middle of nowhere!" Johnathan whispered angrily as he headed to his room his gray eyes flared.

"Johnathan!" He turns and his expression softened as he turned toward her. "I am sorry," she whispered sadly. "I know how you feel. I am sorry," she repeated.

He closed his eyes and winced in pain. "I am tired of hearing that. I do not want you to ever say that to me." He sighed as he headed toward her. "Dad says it every time he looks at me, and when he doesn't say it I can see it in his eyes and it kills me." He gripped the banister tightly, his knuckles turned white and he forced the tears back as whispered, "Good night Lucky I will see you in the morning." He ran up the stairs and shut the door lightly. She followed behind him slowly. She touched his door tenderly before she continued to walk down the hall.

She sighed lightly as she walked out to the balcony. The sun began to rise as she stared at the orange and pink sky while the large mountains tossed a shadow over the grounds. She sighed as she closed the window and curtains. "I just hope things will turn out for the better and not for the worst." Her fingers glided over the brass banister as she walked back to her room.

Chapter Two
Jaire

"Dad it has only been a week since we moved here. Since you *made* us move here!" Johnathan complained as he trudged out of his room. His brown hair slicked back and his gray eyes afire, he wore navy dress pants and a business style white dress shirt. "I don't know why we have to go to this party. It has nothing to do with us, it is about you remember?" He said miserably. He shoved his hands in his pocket in frustration.

"Lucky hurry up!" Her dad called to her impatiently. "Johnathan this is not the time to discuss this. This is a formal dinner so *my family and I* can get use to the scenery and meet new people."

"I still do not want to go to this thing. I rather wait in the car." He folded his arms as he headed down the stairs the creaking of his sister's door made him turn around.

Lucy strolled out of the room gracefully. Her dress was a dazzling pale blue that glided along the floor, and her dark hair was strung up into a small bun at the nape of her neck. She held out her hand and her father to it happily.

"Lucky you look beautiful," her father boomed. He wore a black suit with a matching black bowtie; his light brown hair was parted and brushed neatly.

"Yeah, Lucy you look wonderful," her brother breathed.

"I found this dress in a trunk under my bed. I think it was momma's." She smiled elegantly.

Her father smiled as he reached in his pocket and pulled out a long navy box. "That reminds me. Your mother wanted me to give this to you after she died but I could not part with it for a long time."

She took the box cautiously and ran her fingers over the soft covering. "Oh just stop looking at the box and open it," her father whispered. Her fingers found the latch and opened it and inside the box was a string of pearls.

"Oh Daddy, she use to wear these to every party she went to." Lucy cried.

"Yes, she did and she wanted you to have them." He glanced at his watch and cried in alarm. "Yikes! We have to hurry." He gently pushed them out the door and into the car.

She stared out the window as darkness swirled around her. Shadows clung to the van like leeches trying to suck all happiness and light out of her. Lucy sighed as she concentrated on the empty highway that laid ahead of her, as she gazed at the clean signs she noticed something out of the corner of her eye, a boy.

His long blonde hair hung loosely on his broad shoulders; his back was turned away from her so she could not see his face. He wore a long trench coat despite the warm night and his jeans were ripped and faded. She took one last longing glance at the boy in black as her father sped away, determined to get to the party on time.

Jaire watched the van speed down the road past him. He remembered a girl staring at him. Her eyes pierce through his back; her gaze had caught him off guard. There was something about her presence; it made him feel…warm. *I have got to find her.* He thought. He headed toward the forest when he heard a soft laugh echoing through the night.

"No," He whispered as he raced through the vines and trees trying to escape from the laughter that mocked him. His heart froze as the laughter grew louder and louder. He pushed through bushes and leapt over puddles, he ran blindly through the forest but stopped when he heard laughter and music.

He ducked behind a large pine tree. Cars lined the circle driveway and women in beautiful gowns stepped out of their vehicles and strolled up the large stone steps and disappeared behind stain glass doors. This seemed all too familiar to him, the laughter, the exquisite music, and the splendid food that the punctual waiters served. He could still hear the flighty giggles from ladies and the bellowing chuckles from gentlemen. The sound of the band still echoed inside of his brain, pounding the walls of his already tortured mind. The rich food still left it's sweet taste in the back of his throat and it made him gag.

The mansion loomed in front of him and he could picture the inside: red drapes hung from the windows, rare paintings were plastered over the walls, and tables lined the side with bottles of white wine, accompanied by waiters dressed in black and white tuxes. Yes, he has seen this whole affair over and over in his mind and felt disgusted every time he visited his own memory.

Then something caught his eye, the mini van that had past him on the highway. He watched closely as a man and a boy in matching black suits get out of the van. The man and the boy seemed to be having a disagreement as they walk around the other side of the van. The man opened the passenger side door and a girl stepped out. Her dark hair was in a fancy bun at the base of her neck, and a beautiful pearl necklace was wrapped around her pale throat. She glanced toward the tree and Jaire jumped back as if she could see him. She quickly turned toward the boy and the man and her expression grew stern.

"Daddy, Johnathan, can't we have one outing where you two do not make it a war zone." Lucy pleaded. Lines of worry creased her smooth forehead as she frowned.

"I am sorry honey;" He kissed her forehead and held out his arm, "I will try not to look like an ass. I promise."

"I will try to." Her brother smile weakly. He followed his father's gesture and held out his arm.

"Thank you. I know you do not like this kind of thing Johnathan, but we do need to get out and meet some people." She winced slightly when she saw her brother's eyes darken. She laced her arms through her brother's and her father's arm and together they walked through the door.

The moment she walked though the door she was swept away. A large band played in the corner while people shuffled on the dance floor while holding wineglasses that were filled half way with a dark red wine. A crystal chandelier dangled from the ceiling and candles were lit in the center of each table that lined the sides of the walls. Women wore party dress in an array of colors while the men wore black and white tuxes and blue business suits. It was like a castle from a fairy story to Lucy.

"Chris!" A man over in the corner bellowed. Her father followed the call and met the man.

"Ridge Rogers!" He chuckled. "I have not seen you for a long time. What has it been, ten, fifteen years?"

"Actually it has been twenty years, buddy." Ridge laughed. "What the hell are you doing in the hollers?" His thick accent echoed in Lucy's ears.

"Just getting back to my roots." Her father smiled weakly. "Have you met my kids?" He pushed Johnathan and Lucy toward the chuckling man.

"Hello." Lucy said softly as she shook the man's hand.

"This is my daughter Lucy and my son Johnathan." Johnathan nodded politely.

"You have a beautiful daughter and your son looks just like you." Johnathan turned away, his face contorted into a look of disgust.

"I am going to the restroom, Lucy." Johnathan whispered as he walked away from his father. Tears hid behind her eyes as she watched her brother's anger simmer quietly, he kept his head held high and as he walked his cold eyes looked through the dancers.

"Daddy I need to get some air. Don't worry I will be back soon." She kissed her father on the cheek as she casually strolled out the door. Gracefully nodding and smiling at the people who entered.

Finally, I am out of there. Johnathan is like daddy in so many ways, and it breaks my heart to see them fight, they use to be best friends. She walked across the lawn until she spotted a gazebo in the corner of the property. She headed toward it as if it was a lighthouse and she was a lost ship. She grasped the white railing of the gazebo as she walked in. She let her hair down and wandered around the gazebo. Drops of rain hit the alcove like tears from the heavens.

Jaire stared through the rain he was mesmerized by the girl. He watched her walk out of the shelter and into the pouring rain and she began to dance with the rain, her sky blue dress floated in the night air. He could not take his eyes off of her.

She turned his way and his heart stopped; she headed toward him. Her dark blue eyes pierced right through him; he panicked and scurried back into the woods before she could see him.

He threw himself against a large pine tree once he was sure she could not follow him. The pain ceased from his chest, his breathing slowed as the rain streamed down his body. He long hair fell loose from the leather strap that held his hair from his face. He walked through the woods as if he was lost in a dream. Images of the girl danced in his mind. A small smile found its way to his lips.

He closed his eyes as he walked and opened them to see where his feet had led him. He stood at the bottom step of an old cottage, his old cottage. Jaire walked up the creaky steps of his cottage. The scent of decaying wood and old mothballs inflamed his nose. As he entered the cottage memories flooded his mind when he stared at the remains.

"I have not been here for almost twenty years," he whispered as he ran his slender fingers over a warped pine diner table; dusty china haunted the shattered cabinets. He wandered through each room pursued by memories. He floated as if he was lost in a daze. He stopped in front of a large wood door and inhaled deeply. He turned the knob slowly. Much to his dismay it was locked.

He cried out and rested his back against the door and sighed. Even years later the door remained locked. He clutched a silver pendent that hung around his neck. The pendent had been shattered a long time ago by a girl that had once filled his cold heart with joy and warmth, but after she left only darkness remained. It had all been apart of a great and terrible scheme by a vile and evil woman who wreaked havoc on anyone that dared to cross her path.

A soft cackle echoed throughout the halls of the forgotten cottage. Jaire felt his whole body tense and turn icy cold. "Oh, Jaire you haven't changed a bit." A light gray smoke leaked from the windows and dripped from the ceiling and oozed down the walls creeping like slime.

Jaire's blood ran cold as the smoke encircled his legs and scaled up his body. Fingers formed and stroked his cheek tenderly. He turned away. "Jaire why must you reject me? I am a part of you and always will be." A woman stepped in front of him; her long fiery red curls shook with every turn of her head. She was dressed in a fine black silk dress with a cut that was just above her knee; diamonds laced her neck and fingers; her skin as pale as the moon and her lips as red as blood.

"I am not a part of you anymore," he said coldly. She ran her fingers through his wet hair and sighed softly.

"You see, you need me, you can't live without me. I have what you need and you can't survive without it. I have your heart." She smirked. Her green eyes sparkled in the dark.

"I don't need it to live. I don't need what had happened that had got me in this mess, again. You know where the door is, Esmeralda I do not need to show you." He stood up and walked away.

"Don't you turn your back on me Jaire, I own you and until the end of the world I will. You may shut me out now, but you won't later just like last time. She has returned and she will break your heart again, and you will return to me just like before." She disappeared in a cloud of dust and smoke.

"Some things never change." He grabbed a broom from the closet and swept away the dust. "A century has past and I still am not free." He closed his eyes and inhaled the dusty air.

Chapter Three
Forgotten Dreams

Empty boxes flooded the driveway before the garbage truck came to take them away. Lucy stared at her new room with a glazed expression. The room held all of her possessions, but they seemed out of place on the pink walls and matching pink carpet. Everything in the room seemed too bright and unnatural to her. Life seemed unnatural; her family seemed out of place without her mother to guide them though the day. She had been the glue that held them together.

She sighed as she shut the door. The rain pounded on the roof demanding to be let in. She shuffled down the hall and stopped when she noticed something dangling from the ceiling. She tugged on the rope and stairs fell from the ceiling in a cloud of dust.

"What the heck?" Lucy walked up the steps, her heart beating wildly in her chest as she stared around the dark room. "This must be the attic," she whispered softly.

She found a light switch on the wall. Lighting flashed outside the window. She explored the room. Pictures lay dusty and warped on the floor and leaned against the wall. A large oval rug dominated the floor; the black was faded but the red was bright and vibrant. Her heartbeat quickened as she stepped on it. Her toe snagged the edge of the rug and she tripped.

She looked up and saw a small black book lying on a small footstool. She dusted her knees off and sat on her heels as she opened the book. The pages were worn and yellow, but the black ink was bold. In the inside of the book was a picture of her mother at age sixteen. The diary was her mother's.

"Lucky we're home," her father called. "Where are you?"

"I am in the attic daddy. I will be right down." She grabbed the diary and rushed down the stairs to her room. She tucked the diary safely in her drawer before she ran to see her father and brother.

"Hello Lucky!" Her father beamed. He was dressed in navy dress pants and a white shirt that was unbuttoned at the top.

"Where did you two go?" she asked with a smile. Her father ran his fingers through his hair. She stared at his hand; he wasn't wearing his wedding band only a ring of pale skin remained.

"We just went to the electronic store, Luce, to get an upgrade for my computer." Her brother shrugged coldly and walked away.

"Daddy there is something you are not telling me." She eyed her father suspiciously.

"We just went shopping Lucky it is all right." He walked back to the car. "I have got to go. I will see you two tonight, bye." He kissed her on the cheek. "Tell your brother that I am sorry," he said sadly.

"I will daddy. Drive safely. I love you." She hugged him one last time. A small tear ran down her cheek. *"I am sorry's" seem to be replacing I love you's and tears are replacing smiles.* She hated the silence that fell between her father and brother.

She slowly walked up the stairs to her brother's room. She knocked softly. Her brother's cool voice answered. "Come in."

"Hey," she whispered.

"Hey." He put his headphones beside his computer. "I am sorry I thought you were Dad. What's the matter Lucy, you look like you have been crying."

"Don't worry I haven't. So how is it going?" she asked as she stared at her brother's room. Posters of his favorite bands littered the wall and books were neatly stacked on his desk. She flopped down on his bed and flipped through one of his books.

"Nothing's different. We are still stuck here and dad's..." He sighed. "You will find out tonight. Things are just changing so fast and I can't keep up. Dad wants me to be like him and I can't, I do not want to either." He sighed as he turned off his computer. "Mom always said 'children are only as similar to their parents as they want to be'."

"He just wants you to have a good life Johnathan." She looked up from the book. Her brother's face was cold and expressionless.

"You sound just like him Lucy. You always stand up for him." He sighed. "I have work to do. Please go Luce." She stared out the window the sun was shining but the air was cold in Johnathan's room.

"I love you, Johnathan, and so does daddy and we always will no matter how much you push us away," she whispered as he closed the door. He was shutting everyone out including her. *Mom where are you?* She thought desperately.

She walked outside into the sunshine. Her bike waited for her in the garage. A thin layer of dust had settled on the frame, she had not ridden it for over a year, since her mother's death. They use to ride together to the park, the dairy queen, to the store, or anywhere they wanted to, she felt free and happy when they were together.

She lifted her leg over the seat and sat down. She felt the chip on her shoulder being lifted as she rode faster and faster down the road. Pure ecstasy flowed through her veins as she let go of the handlebars and flew down the road. Her heart pounded in her chest as she closed her eyes. The wind whipped through her long hair. She felt free and wonderful. When she opened her eyes reality sink in as the sun began to set. She was miles away from home and alone and traveling full speed down a steep hill.

"No! Stop!" Her brakes just made a screech and she could not stop. "Help! Someone please help me!" She closed her eyes as her bike headed head long into a large tree.

Lucy waited for the pain but she felt none. A gentle deep voice spoke to her. "Are you all right miss?" She opened her eyes and realized she was on the ground.

"Yeah. Where am I?" She stared up at her savior. It was pitch black and all she could see was his long blonde hair floating in the wind.

"You are about a half a mile from the main road. What are you doing out here so late you should get back home before your mother worries about you," he whispered sternly.

She felt her heart turn ice as a tear slid down her cheek. "You do not have to worry about that my mother is dead," she whispered bitterly.

"I am sorry. I have a phone inside if you like to call home," he asked gently. His voice was warm and welcoming.

"No one is home right now. My father is at a meeting and my brother can not come and get me because dad has the only car. I will head back home. Thank you for helping me." She shook his hand and grabbed her bike and started to leave when she felt a hand on her shoulder.

"I will go with you. You shouldn't go out in the dark. There are creatures that lurk behind the trees and mountains." His hands were cold.

"I am not afraid. I can handle myself." She pushed his hand off of her shoulder.

"Like you handled yourself with the bike?" He whispered; his voice was concerned and, yet, indifferent and cool.

"I will call my brother and hope my father is home." She pulled out her cell phone. The line was busy. "Oh crap. The line is busy."

Rain sprang from the clouds and drenched them. "Just when I thought things could not get worse." She laughed sarcastically. "God opens the clouds and cries 'I hate you Lucy'." She covered her head with her bag.

"Come inside," he whispered.

This is not what he had planned to do; why did she have to come and fall into his lap. He heard the door shut behind him. He turned around and looked at her. Her dark hair was tied in a ponytail and her clothes were soaked. But what that struck him was her eyes. They were the darkest blue he had ever seen.

"Make yourself comfortable. By the way I am Jaire. Jaire DeCrothro." His smile was small and strained.

"I am Lucy Montgomery." She graciously took his hand. Images flashed though his head as he stared into her eyes. A strange warmth entered his body; he turned away before he lost the cold that had, for so long protected him from the cruel heartless world.

She took a seat on the large chair near the window; her body shook from the cold. He could feel her watching him from the corner of her eye as he left the room. He came back with a large black wool blanket. "Here take it." He walked to the kitchen to make some coffee.

Once he was out of the room, he closed his eyes and breathed softly. There was something about this girl that shattered every piece of glass in his hollow heart and she did it with a turn of her head. *Don't get to close, Bucco. Remember why you came back, to get away from everyone.* He thought to himself. *Don't get to attached.*

The kettle whistled and he jumped from his dark thoughts. He made the coffee and carried it into the living room. He turned to hand a steaming cup to her, but she was fast asleep. He placed the cup on the table and pulled the blanket up to her neck.

"This is not going to end this night I just know it." He laid back in his chair and watched the rain trickle down the window. There was something about her that made him wonder how life would have been if he had never met Esmeralda. All of his dreams may have come true, but he threw it all away with one single selfish impractical wish. She controlled his body and kept his heart in a little wooden box, but she could not control his mind and his thoughts and all of the forgotten dreams that trailed behind him.

Chapter Four
Little Black Book

Lucy awoke in her bed with a headache. She was draped in a black wool blanket. Memories of last night flooded her aching head. "How did I get here?" she whispered as she crawled out of bed.

"Dad came and picked you up." Johnathan stood in the doorway; his light hair shone in the morning light and his face was hidden in the shadows his voice was bitter.

"When?" She yawned.

"Last night, he saw your number on the id and called you back to see what was the matter and that guy that found you picked up and told us where to find you. Lucy, I am sorry that I snapped at you yesterday."

"It is all right Johnathan." She yawned again.

"Dad's waiting for you in the kitchen. We were really worried last night. I am sorry I was on the computer. Why didn't you tell me you were going for a ride?" He asked softly.

"I needed the time alone. I better go meet daddy," she whispered. She hugged her brother. "Aren't you coming?"

"I met him last night," he whispered bitterly.

She walked down the stairs and when she was halfway down she heard a woman's giggle and her father's deep laugh. She rushed down the stairs and came face to face with a woman who had red hair and dazzling catlike green eyes. Lucy grew dizzy.

"Daddy who is this?" she choked.

"Lucky this is Isabelle. I met her last night after I saw your number on the ID. It was strange; she was stranded on the road after her car went over the side of the mountain. She is very lucky to be alive. She is going to stay with us for awhile, I hope you do not mind." Her father's words were vague as she stared at this woman that stood in her mother's kitchen, wearing her mother's robe.

"I hope we can become friends." Her smile was shallow and cold. She held out her hand and Lucy shook it, it was as cold as ice. Her body trembled when she stared into Isabelle's green eyes; she felt like she was suffocating the longer that Isabelle held onto her hand. The world grew dark as she fell to the floor. She could hear her father yelling for her to wake up but he seemed so far away.

She rubbed her forehead and sat up. Her father rushed to her side. "Are you all right Lucky?"

"Daddy don't worry I just need to get some fresh air. I will be back soon." She walked to the door. She could feel Isabelle's cold stare pierce her back. She shut the door behind her and stood on the porch until the sun warmed her cold body. Then she remembered the blanket and ran back inside to grab the blanket.

"Honey what is the matter?" She heard her father call to her.

"I just forgot something." She stuffed the blanket in her pack and a few books before she left again. She walked down the paved road, birds chirped and the small creek babbled beside her. The air seemed cleaner and cleared her cluttered mind with every step she took.

Finally she arrived at her destination, the small cottage where she had found shelter during the storm. She took a deep breath before she walked through the rickety gate. The sound of the porch steps creaking beneath her was the only sound that she heard. She knocked on the door softly. When no one answered she banged on the door until it opened with a soft creak.

"Hello? Anyone here? Jaire? I am here just to bring back the blanket." She folded the blanket neatly on the couch and wrote her name and phone number along with a simple thank you. She walked out of the house and spotted a small gazebo on a hill she headed toward it.

Once she was there she pulled out the books she brought with her. A small black book fell out of her bag and onto the floor. She picked it up and realized it was her mother's diary. She flipped through the pages and when she reached the end she spotted a small flap on the back inside cover. She opened it and pulled out a small pendent. She ran her fingers over it; it was black with a small red jewel in the middle but it was only half of a pendent. She stood up and the diary fell on the ground when she picked it up again a note fell out.

To my darling daughter Lucy:
If you are reading this I must have left this world. This pendent was given to me when I was sixteen by someone who I had really cared about. I want you to take it and keep it close to your heart it will keep you safe when I can not. Love is not always the path that is easiest, but do not let it blind you in the intensity of its light. A heart does not always have to be in bloom to fall in love, it can be old as time, but give it a chance and things will work out in the end.

I wish for you to have a happy life full of adventure. As I stare into your beautiful dark eyes and I know that you will go further than I ever did. I want you to watch out for your brother and father. They will need you. I love you my little dark angel.

Love Always,
Your mother, Lilliana Montgomery
PS There is another letter enclosed for Johnathan. I love you both more than life itself.

Tears streamed down her face as the rain poured from the heavens. She pressed the letter and pendent close to her chest. The sharp edges pierced the palm of her hand but she felt no pain as the blood ran down to her wrist. She fastened the clasp on the necklace.

She stood up quickly and threw her things back into her pack but when she was about to leave her vision blurred and the world swirled around her. The man with long blonde hair stared at her. Then the world went black.

Jaire stared at her. *Not her again. What is it with her?* He carried her through the rain and into his cottage. He kindled the fire and wrapped the blanket around her once again. The kettle whistled loudly.

"Who are you?" He whispered as he stared at her. Her dark hair fell across her pale face. "Why do you keep coming here and why do I keep saving you?"

He impulsively pushed the strand away from her eyes. His fingers stroked her cheek tenderly.

He pulled his hand away as her eyes fluttered open. She shot up. "Where am I?" she whispered. Her back was turned to him. Her hand went to a necklace around her neck.

"You are at my cottage again," Jaire whispered. She turned toward him. Her dark eyes searching his face. "I found you in the alcove on the hill. Are you all right?"

"Yes, I am fine. I am sorry for intruding. I just came back to return the blanket and then I was on my way home then I saw the gazebo and decided to read a little. Then it started to rain and..." She stared down at her hand. Dried blood covered her palm and wrist.

Jaire shook his head. *Why didn't I see that before?* He calmly walked to the kitchen and came back with a bandage. "Please you have already done enough for me. I better go." She sighed and added bitterly, "Before dad and Isabelle worry."

"No, let me help you." He took her hand gently. He wrapped the bandage around her hand. She smiled shyly.

"How long have you been living here?" she asked him.

"I just moved back last week." His tone was bitter. "You?"

"My father," She rose and walked toward the window, "moved my twin brother and me after my mother died. She died last year in a car accident. Ever since then things have been changing so quickly and no one is the way they use to be. Johnathan, my brother, use to smile all the time and now the only thing to cross his lips is a frown. Even daddy has changed. He tries so hard to make things like they were but they are not the same."

"Last night my father met a woman who is now staying with us. I want to like her, but every time I look at her my heart turns to ice. I just want him to be happy." She rubbed her neck as she watched the rain pelt the grass.

"Life is full of changes. If everything remained the same what kind of life would that be?" Jaire whispered. He watched her close her eyes and fight back tears.

"But why does life have to take the most important things away?" She whispered bitterly, "and replace them with something entirely different?"

"To make us stronger. Loss is something that everyone deals with and it is what you do that makes you who you are. It can make or break you." He walked toward her. Silent tears ran down her cheek. "I am sorry for your loss, but you cannot let it overtake you and destroy you."

"I am tired of hearing those words!" She turned to face him. Her eyes grew darker and her hands shook with anger. "I hate those words. *I am sorry.* I hear them every night before I go to bed, I hear my father tell my brother that every day and it is killing me." Jaire wrapped his arms around her shaking shoulders as she cried into his shirt.

She pushed him away gently. "I apologize for disturbing you. I am sorry I lost it like that. I better go. I promise I will leave you alone. Good bye Jaire." She tossed the blanket at him and grabbed her pack as she rushed out the door and into the pouring rain.

She was half way down the road when Jaire realized what had happened. He felt a small burning pain in his chest and looked to see what was the matter. His pendent was glowing red. He grasped it, but it was hot. There was more to her than meets the eye.

Chapter Five

Isabelle

"Dear you are soaked." Lucy trudged up the steps. Her clothes were drenched and her hand burned with pain. "Hurry inside before you catch your death." Isabelle ushered her in. Isabelle rushed to the kitchen and came back with two steaming cups.

"I am all right Isabelle." Lucy muttered. "You do not have to do anything. Where is daddy?" She looked around the room.

"He went looking for you. He didn't want you alone in the cold. I have lived here all of my life and it has never rained as much as it is now. It is quite strange. Here have some peppermint tea; it will warm you up." She pushed a small pink teacup Lucy's way.

"Thank you." She smiled weakly. The pendent grew hot and burned her skin. She dropped the cup. Shards of porcelain scattered on the tile floor. Her hands shook; it felt as if the earth was moving beneath her feet. She knelt down to pick the pieces up.

"It is all right. Dear are you okay? Don't worry I will…" Isabelle's voice trailed off. "Dear what is that around your neck?"

"Oh," She covered the pendent with her injured hand. "It was something my mother gave me." Isabelle could not take her eyes off of Lucy.

"May I touch it?" She spoke as if she was in a trance.

"No." She tucked it safely in her shirt. "I better change out of these wet clothes. I will have that tea with you later." She ran up to her room. When she passed her brother's room she found him sitting at his computer staring mindlessly at the screen. She reached into her pocket and pulled out the envelope addressed to Johnathan. She knocked on the door softly.

"Come in Luce." He turned off the monitor and removed his headphones. "What's the matter?"

"Yesterday I found mom's old diary and today I was looking though it and I found a letter addressed to me…and one to you." She handed him the letter. He stared at her with cold eyes.

"Lucy this is not a joke. Dad says mom hasn't been here since we were born…" He clasped the envelope tightly.

"Johnathan I would never lie to you. Just read it." She hugged her brother and walked out of the room. Once she was in her room she changed and laid on her bed to read her mother's diary. Pictures of her family through the years smiled at her on her dresser; she cradled the picture of them that was taken a week before the crash, everyone was smiling even Johnathan. What had made him turn so cold in so short of time?

Lucy held her letter in her hand. She noticed the date that the letter was written, it had been written three months before the crash. *How can that be? Dad said she hadn't been here since they were born.*

A soft knock on the door brought her back to reality. Johnathan stared at the carpet, tears dripped from his face. "Johnathan? What is the matter?"

He handed her the letter. "I can not read it. Will you please read it to me? I do not want to disappoint her." He sobbed softly.

Dear Johnny,

Life is not always easy and things have to change. Do not let your father control you, he loves you and means well, but you must live your own life. Remember I will always love you for who you are. You are my perfect little boy and will be no matter how old you are. Life is full of surprises, but do not just shrug them away there is more than meets the eye. Take care of your sister together you two are stronger than you think. I love you more than the air that I breathe, my dear Johnny.

Love,
Your mother, Lilliana

Lucy wrapped her arms around her brother who cried into her shoulder. "There, there. Johnathan everything will work out."

He pushed her away and whispered sorrowfully, "Things will never be all right. The cut is too deep, Luce, the pain is just too real."

"Mom loved you, Daddy loves you and so do I; it will all work out as long as there is love." She held his hand.

"Lucy stop living in a dream world, love isn't always enough. Love is just a word it no longer has a meaning to me." He pushed her hand away and walked out of the room. *How can life be so cruel and heartless? Why?*

"To make us stronger. Loss is something that everyone deals with and it is what you do that makes you who you are. It can make or break you." Jaire's words echoed in her mind.

Isabelle had been staying with Lucy and her family for over a week. The night before they went to a fancy restaurant and she watched with disgust how Isabelle threw herself at her father.

Isabelle was waiting for Lucy the next morning at the dinner table. Her dark red hair cascaded down to her slender pale shoulders. Her bright green eyes were cold and full of fake happiness. "Dear I want to talk to you. Come and sit with me." She motioned toward a chair.

"Where is father?" she asked as she took a seat.

"He went out and wanted me to talk to you. He is very concerned about you and wants you and your brother to have a full happy life, he loves you both very much and he wants me to ask you if…"

A groan echoed throughout the room. Johnathan walked in, his light hair was unkempt and his expression was deadly. "He does not love us, if he did he would have never asked you to stay here. I want nothing to do with his new life. He never asked us to move here so I want nothing to do with him." He rushed out the door and slammed it behind him.

"Your father asked me to be his wife. Is that all right?" she asked with a menacing smile.

"I do not know. Just give me a little time to think about this. He just met you. My father has a fear of commitment, it took him several years to ask my mother to marry him, but it only took a week to ask you? This is such bull-"

"Do not use that tone with me. We are getting married even if you do not like it. So, darlin'', get use to it." Isabelle stormed off to her room.

Lucy clasped the pendent as she ran out of the house and ran until she couldn't anymore. Her breathing was ragged and painful. She slid down the side of a tree and fought the tears that were waiting for her on the edge. She held her head in her hands.

"Not her again," Jaire whispered as he watched her from his window. The pendent around his neck grew hot every time he looked at her. He walked out the door and right back into her eyes.

"Oh, I am sorry. This time I really did not mean to intrude. I just need to get away from…I just needed to get away that is all." She slowly stood up. He pulled a small handkerchief from his back pocket and wiped her tears away.

"What's the-" he moaned as he grabbed his chest. He fell to the ground. The burning increased. "Just go. I can handle myself," he whispered painfully.

"No, you would not let me go. It is now my turn to help you." She threw his arm around her shoulders. Once they were in the house she laid him on the couch.

"Oh, Jaire you have a girlfriend." Esmeralda's voice echoed throughout the empty walls of his mind. "How long will this one last before she abandons you once she finds out she can never keep you? What are you going to do to her if she does not understand?" He felt her cold fingers on his skin. He could smell her suffocating perfume but she wasn't there she was only in his mind. "Are you going to kill again Jaire?"

"NO!!!" he cried. His eyes were wild with hate.

"You can not control your emotions that is why you came to me isn't it Jaire? You wanted her so bad. You told me you needed her or you would die but she was just like the rest of them. Those foolish girls do not understand your pain, but I do. Come back to me and I will give you the world together we will be unstoppable."

"Never!" he yelled.

"Remember I have your heart and I control you." She wrapped her arms around his neck. "I love you, she doesn't. She doesn't even know what it means."

"Leave me alone! Go away!" he yelled as he sat upright on the couch. He felt someone call to him. Lucy's soft voice called to him.

"Jaire it is all right." She stroked his forehead as she laid a cold rag where her hand was.

"What happened?" he moaned.

"You blacked out. You were yelling and screaming in your sleep, are you all right?" she whispered as she poured him a cup of coffee.

"Yeah it was just a bad dream. Thank you."

"No problem. Think of it as me repaying you for helping me out." She knelt beside him on the floor. "What was your dream about?" she asked casually.

"My past," he muttered with disdain. He stared out the window; the sun pushed the clouds away. "How long was I out?"

"A few hours." She fingered something around her neck. His pendent burned but he ignored the pain. *This girl is trouble. The pendent has never reacted this way before.* "What are you holding?"

"Oh this?" She pulled it out of her shirt and fingered it with care. "I found it in my mother's diary. She wanted me to have it." Jaire could not take his eyes off of it. He clasped his pendent; the edges were sharp and the jewel scalded his palm. *I knew it! She is trouble.*

"That is very exquisite, but it is broke." He touched it, but she pulled it away.

"I have been looking for the other half but I could not find it. Mother did not mention it too much." she said thoughtfully.

"What was your mother's name?"

"Lilliana. Why?"

Lilliana. Lilliana. That name had haunted him for years. Lilliana was everything that meant nothing to him anymore, but she had possessed his heart for so short of time.

"Did you know her?" she asked as she stroked the pendent.

"No," he quickly lied. He had to get her out of his house and out of her life. "I think you should go." He stood up and walked toward the door.

"I can't! I do not want to go back to that hideous woman!" she said hotly.

"Why not?" he said.

"Because…Never mind you have no idea what I am going through. So I will leave you alone." She grabbed her coat and ran out the door. Rain followed her every step.

Chapter Six
Painful Tears

"How could he do that?" she cried as she stumbled through the rain. When she was on her porch she found Isabelle waiting for her. Her hands on her thin hips and her lips were twisted in a horrifying smirk.

"I told you that you could not run from me. He will reject you like he has to the women in your family. He is cursed." She turned back into the house.

"What?!" she cried as she grabbed Isabelle's cold arm.

"He rejects everything that comes in his life. So do not even try, the blood that flows through his veins is only ice. He feels nothing, but his own selfish pain. You can never keep him; he belongs to someone else," she whispered in Lucy's ear smugly. She walked out of the house with only a few parting words: "Watch your back because if you do not you will find yourself with a knife in it. Bye dear," she whispered sweetly.

She fell back into one of the chairs as her anger soared. The pendent around her neck glowed brightly. "She is the one who should watch her back," she said irately.

"Jaire." A soft whisper echoed throughout the cottage. "Who is your little girlfriend?" He felt the hair on the back of his neck stand up and his skin prickle.

"I have no idea what you are talking about Esmeralda." He continued to read flipping through the worn pages.

"I saw her." Esmeralda snuggled close to him. "Does she mean anything to you?" She ran her finger down his cheek.

"She means nothing to me," he muttered coldly. "Remember I feel nothing, I have no heart."

"You are right Jaire." She pressed her hand against his chest. "I have it. So what if I got rid of the little pest."

He threw her to the ground. "No! Do not even dare to harm a hair on her head," he cried.

"Oh, so she does mean something to you?" She smiled happily and mischief sparkled in her eyes.

"No. Do you know whose daughter she is? Do you?" he cried.

"I do not know." A wicked smile crossed her lips. "Lilliana Ward's daughter."

"Yes, and I do not want to get into that mess again. Her whole family has been nothing, but trouble for me." He grasped the pendent.

"She is not like her mother. She is weak and easy to control. Her heart is too frail and her mind is full of fear and regret."

Jaire turned away. The sky grew dark and lighting lit up the sky, but no rain came. "That is what you said about her grandmother and look what happened to me. I have eternity and for her to thank. Death never knocks at my door no matter how hard I listen."

Lucy sped down the road. Her bike creaked and groaned the harder she pedaled. The clouds cried in agony the closer she got to his house. She had to know the truth.

After Isabelle left her house she ran to the attic and searched through the old photo books but she found nothing until she referred to her mother's diary and found a passage dated July 27, 1981.

Dear Diary,

I have found the man of my dreams. His name is Jaire DeCrothro. He is like no other boy. He understands my powers and embraces them. We do everything together. We ride bikes and spend long hours at his cottage down the road. He gave me a pendent. He is a gentleman unlike that arrogant

Christopher Montgomery. I have to hurry because I am meeting Jaire tonight for dinner. He says he has something to tell me. I hope he wants to marry me. I have wished for nothing else.
   Lilliana Ward

Her parents started dating July 31, 1981 so she read the next entry.

Dear Diary,
   Jaire broke my heart. He is cold and bitter as the wind in January. I threw the pendent he gave me against the alcove and it shattered, like my heart. He lied to me. I will make him pay. Mother warned me about him, why didn't I listen? She said she knew him when she was my age. I thought she was just kidding, but he told me...

Her writing stopped. Lucy had to know what Jaire had told her mother. Her pendent glowed through the dark. A strange power surged through her as she threw her bike on the ground. She opened the door to find Jaire standing in the middle of the living room shaking.

"Why have you come? I had told you to leave!" he cried painfully. The pendent on his chest burned. Esmeralda left her impression on him. He was caged in her cold grasp.

"I want answers and I want them now!" She tossed her mother's diary at his feet.

"You told me you did not know her. You lied to me."

"Where did you get this?" he whispered. A picture of him and Lilliana fell out of the cover. The pendent glowed merrily around Lilliana's neck.

"It is none of your damn business!" she cried. "What did you tell her?" she whispered calmly.

His eyes were locked on the picture. Hot tears rolled down his face. Memories, happy memories broke through the gates of his mind. He remembered her beautiful smile and the way she made his heart feel light. He loved the way she made him feel happy and the way she brought the light back into his life. But that was long ago, before he gave his heart to Esmeralda.

"Tell me what you told her! Why did you hurt her so?" Tears continued to fall from his eyes.

"Sit down, you need to know the truth about your past. Your mother was not what she appeared." He took a deep breath.

"What do you mean? Was she a witch?"

"No, not really. She could control the weather." He sighed as he held the picture. "She made my life better. She made the rain go away. I guess I should start at the beginning…"

"Long ago over a century I lived here with my family, my mother, brother, and sister. My father was killed when he left for Maine; a highwayman robbed and killed him. We were probably the wealthiest family for miles, we settled here for the peace and quiet. We lived fine for a few years until I met Lucinda Ward, your great grandmother; I fell in love with her the first time I saw. She was beautiful, like your mother.

I wanted her. I thought I needed her, I tried everything to get her attention, but she saw through my arrogant advances. I was finally at my wit's end when I met Esmeralda, at the time she was like an angel or a godsend. She told me everything I wanted to hear, and I was a sucker for every smoke and mirror trick she pulled.

So I sold my soul to her in exchange that I would have Lucinda. I searched and searched for her, but she had left town. She was engaged to another man, Johnathan Rojas of Michigan. When I went back to Esmeralda's home she just cooed and smiled. I once again fell for her tricks; she told me she could give me eternity without pain.

But it was all a lie. There is no such thing as a life without pain. I drove everyone away. My family and friends left because they thought I had sold my soul to the devil, because I never aged. I will look like I am twenty forever, but my mind is old and as alone as the moon.

I could not bare the silence any longer so I left. I went to Paris, Japan, and Russia; I travel the seven seas. I searched for wars to fight. I watched brave men around me die, but I could not. I delivered the news to the families of the dead, I watched them cry I could feel their pain, it should have been me.

In the year of '81 I came back home and that is when I met her, Lilliana Ward, she said she changed her last name because she liked the sound of it better than Lilliana Rojas. We had the best summer. Yes, life was good, I wish I could go back to that moment and freeze it but as all good things have to come to an end this sure did.

Esmeralda came back to claim what was hers when Lilliana came over. She watched Esmeralda kiss me through the window." He pulled something out from under his shirt. "She threw the pendent that I gave her against the gazebo were we had spent long warm days reading. It shattered and she kept half of it, as a memory for her that all men are not as good as they seem, she told me once she was back home she was going to throw it into the river.

When I tried to explain what happened long ago she called me a liar and ran back home and into the arms of that pompous idiot Christopher Montgomery. That night I gave Esmeralda my broken heart and she cursed me to never feel again and I wanted it. I had lost someone important to me. Once Lilliana left she took the sun away from me, ever since then I have lived in darkness. I left again, but with Esmeralda by my side I did some things that I am not proud of. After a few years I came back here and abandoned her. I swore I would live here for the rest of eternity without anyone, until you came along."

His tears splashed onto the photograph. "Did you love her?"

"Who? Your mother, yes."

"Not my mother, Esmeralda?" Lucy asked ethereally.

"I would never! She used me. She controlled me, I was her puppet and she never forgot to remind me," he whispered bitterly.

"Why did you give her the pendent?"

"What?" he asked. "I gave her my heart." He held the broken pendent in the palm of his hand.

Lucy pulled her pendent out from under her shirt. "I thought she said she threw it into the river." He fingered it.

"No, she didn't. Here take it, you need it more than I do. Thank you for explaining everything. I will leave you now. You do not have to worry about me, live your life the way you want, alone," she whispered coldly as she headed toward the door.

Jaire took a deep breath when she shut the door. *I have lost another.* He held onto the pendent. *Everything has gone wrong, so wrong.*

"You are so right Jaire you have lost her. Come back to me forget her and her family they mean nothing to you anymore." Esmeralda called to him. He bowed his head and nodded gently.

He stared at her with cold eyes. "I will come back to you on one condition: no more killing. I can not do it anymore. I will not. My heart will not allow me to."

"But Jaire I have your heart." Esmeralda held onto his arm.

"No, she does." He threw the pendent on the table.

Chapter Seven
Dreams are at an end

Her back rested upon the tall oak in her backyard. Her tears mixed with the rain. He never loved her. Every time he looked at her he had thought of her mother. "I had been so stupid. I never want to fall in love again." She held her mother's letter close to her heart. "I know now why you hated him momma." She stared at the picture of Jaire and her mother.

"Mother never hated him, Luce." Johnathan stood in front of her with an umbrella.

"How do you know?" she asked hotly.

"Remember when we were little she told us about a boy who could never die and whose life was so dark even Satan felt sorry for him until a beautiful princess came, and brought the light back into his life?" He sat close to her.

"No and I do not want to remember it," she cried.

"You are going to listen. I do not care if you do not want to. A girl I once knew said 'I will never give up on you no matter how hard you push me away,' and I want that girl back. I want my sister back," he whispered imploringly.

"I am sorry Johnathan, but she is long gone. I have got to go inside, I am cold." She started to stand up when Johnathan grabbed her arm and pulled her down.

"You are not leaving until you hear the story. Long ago…

In the hills of Kentucky there lived a boy. He had once lived with his family until he met a beautiful girl her name was Lucinda, he had fallen madly in lust with her. She was beautiful and very kind. He tried every thing to get her attention but nothing work. So the night before her wedding the boy went to the local fortuneteller. Her red hair burn and her green eyes sent shivers down his spine but he begged her to help him get the fair Lucinda to be his wife, and not the Prince Johnathan's. The fortune teller just smiled and said:

"You want her and I can give her to me if you give me your soul." The boy quickly agreed not knowing the consequences if he should fail. He ran back to his town to find Lucinda, but she was gone, she had left during the night with her Prince.

He left the town after his family and friends abandoned him because he never aged. For years he searched for wars to fight, but he could not stand telling the families of the dead soldiers that they had died. He watched their pain and cried with them wishing it were him that had died instead of those brave men.

Once the fighting had ceased he returned home to the cottage. It had grown dusty and dirty but it was home. There was one room in the cottage that he has not been able to open since he sold his soul his mother locked it and threw away the key. But he continued to live in the cottage. He lived in darkness; his ancient mind was full of somber thoughts and forgotten dreams until he met the modest and sweet Lilly.

She was a beautiful princess who had gotten caught in the rain and sought shelter in a gazebo on the top of a hill. He watched her from his window and his icy heart began to melt. He ran out to help her with her bag. She started to run away from home because her father was forcing her to marry Christopher who was a pompous man.

Once she looked into his dark green eyes she knew she was in love. He made her smile and she brought the light back into his heart. She chased away all of the shadows in his mind. They did everything together, they went to parties, and they went bike riding, and danced in the rain. One night after a very extravagant party he gave her a beautiful pendent. She knew she loved him that very night and always will love him.

But one raining day in July he told her the truth that he could never ever die. She cried and called him a liar. She threw the pendent against the tree and when she was about to throw her half into the river she could not because even though she wanted to hate him she could not help, but love him so she kept the half. When she got home he clothes were drenched and Christopher was waiting in the hall he kindly gave her his jacket. When she looked into his gray eyes she saw something that she had not seen before. She saw compassion, truth, and honesty. A few years later they were married and had a pair of beautiful twins a girl and a boy.

Lucy you see she never hated him. She was mad because she could not keep him; she was upset because she could not accept who he was." Her brother hugged her close. "She wanted you to find him. She hoped that you would accept him and bring back the light."

"How do you know? That was just a story Johnathan, momma told us hundreds of them. They are beautiful fairy tales, but this not a fairy tale this is real life and there is no riding off into the sunset with Prince Charming," she whispered bitterly.

He pulled something from his pocket. "This is the other half of the letter. The one I did not want you to see. She told me about him. She told me about the stories. I would have never remembered them Lucy if it weren't for you finding this letter."

"Yeah and look where it got me Johnathan. I am sitting here in the rain listening to fairy tales and wishing they would come true. I wish I could momma could come back and make it all better but she can't and no piece of paper is going to fix that."

"There is a way Luce. It is only a matter of thought and need. Come with me." He held out his hand to help his sister up. "Ever since Dad and I went into one of those shops I have been researching ancient spells and things like that because I had found this spell of some sort and it can summon spirits. So I looked into it more and I found that in the late nineteenth century witch hunters had come across a whole bunch of sorceress, and they some how summoned the dead mother of one man. It might be a whole lot of gibber gabber but I hope it isn't. I have to get a few things from my room, but the attic will be the best place to summon mom." They rushed into the house.

"I hope that this works." After they got the papers from Johnathan's room they headed toward the attic. When Lucy opened the door to the attic they found their father tied to a chair and a woman standing over him.

"Isabelle why are you doing this to me?" her father asked weakly.

"I am not Isabelle my name is Esmeralda."

"Why are you doing this?"

"Because of your darling daughter. She will be looking for you and I am waiting for her to arrive she has to meet my new friend." Esmeralda laughed lightly.

"What are you going to do to her?" her father cried.

"What I had planned to do the moment I saw her with Jaire, I intend to put her out of her misery because now I have him back." She laughed again.

"Don't you harm a hair on her head you evil witch!" Esmeralda backhanded Lucy's father. Lucy could feel her father's pain.

"Da-." Johnathan covered her mouth quickly.

"Let's get out of here Luce." Johnathan whispered in her ear. "We can summon mom in the gazebo." He removed his hand from her mouth.

"But I can not leave dad. Look at him." She watched Esmeralda laugh as she smacked him.

"He can take care of himself. Let's go Lucy," he whispered bitterly.

"No, I got him into this mess and I intend to get him out of it." She crept up the stairs. She ducked behind boxes. She could almost reach her father's bonds when she stepped on a mousetrap. "Oww!" she cried softly.

"Lucy get out of here. She wants to kill you," her father pleaded softly. Small drops of blood dripped from his mouth as he spoke.

"I know and I am not leaving without you." She started to untie the ropes when she felt a cold hand reach behind her neck and pull her from the safety of the shadows.

"Look what stumbled into my world." Esmeralda laughed. Her eyes stared into her soul and froze her mind briefly.

"Let me go and let my father go," she cried. "You have Jaire what more do you want?"

"I want him entirely and I can not have it with you still in this world. First I want to have some fun with you." She struck Lucy in the back of the head with a blunt object.

"Leave her alone! What did she do to you?" her father cried.

"It was just not her, but her mother! They need to be punished and since Lilliana isn't here I will just have to make do with her."

"What? Lilliana did not even know this boy!" her father cried weakly as he stared at his unconscious daughter.

"Yes, she did and he is no boy. He is over a hundred years old. You are lucky that she met him or you would have never married your darling wife. You are lucky he broke her heart or Lucy would never exist!" she hissed and laughed cruelly as she watched his face pale.

Johnathan crouched down into the shadows as he slowly slipped out of the attic. *I have to find that guy.* He scurried through the house as quick and quiet as a mouse. Once he was outside he ran down the road at full speed. He could still hear Lucy's cry inside his head when she had looked at him. She needed Jaire and he needed her, he was sure of it.

He found the cottage that his mother had described. He busted open the door and found nothing. Jaire was not there. "Where the hell are you!? Can't you be here when she really needs you!?" He opened every door.

He ran to the gazebo. "Where are you? Where is the almighty boy that my mom talked about? Where is he, huh? She loves you, you know!" Johnathan cried angrily. He threw his hands up and screamed and cursed Jaire's name.

"There is no need to shout. Esmeralda might hear you." A cool voice came from the shadows.

"You really fear her?" Johnathan asked bitterly. His heart pounded in his chest as he stared at Jaire, he could feel his anger quickly rise as he watched him move.

"I have no feelings except hatred. I feel nothing but pain." He walked out from the shadows. His once dark green eyes were lifeless and his blonde hair was thin and weak and hung limply in the small strip of leather.

"All you feel is self-pity," he cried. "Do you care that Esmeralda is taking over your life?"

"I have no life to live; it died long ago I am just a shell." He whispered.

"Do you care that my father is in trouble?" Johnathan murmured.

"Why should I?" he muttered callously. "He took Lilly from me."

"Lucy is going to die and all you can do is cling to your hatred and self-pity. I have no idea what my sister and mother saw in you. I see you as a coward." Johnathan yelled bitterly. His hands shook as he spoke; he could barely breathe.

"What is the matter with Lucy?" Jaire snapped out of his weakened daze.

"She is going to be killed by that woman if you do not do anything." Johnathan cried.

"Take me to her." Jaire and Johnathan rushed down the road. They ran in silence. The mountains seemed to hold their breath as the pair neared the house.

Chapter Eight
"Forgive me"

She was tied to a chair; her wrists bled from the rope that was cutting into her skin. Esmeralda smacked her until her head was bleeding, but she still remained quiet. She could no longer feel any pain except the ache of her shattered heart.

"Do you know why he chose me over you? You are weak!" She grasped Lucy's hair tightly. "You do not understand him and never will. You are too much like your mother, flighty and worthless. She ran straight into your father's arms after Jaire told her the truth. She could not handle him being different and neither can you. He doesn't love you and he will never. He belongs to me." She threw Lucy against the wall. The ropes broke when she landed against a small letter opener. She moaned softly.

"Your mother just used him for a good time and look what happened, his heart broke and then he gave it to me," she said grimly.

"Then why do you want to kill me if you already have his heart?" Lucy whispered weakly. She knelt against the wall. Blood streamed down her face and arms. Her heart was faintly beating against the wall of her chest. Esmeralda picked her up by her hair.

"Because I *had* it but now you have it." Esmeralda threw Lucy back down to the ground.

"I have no idea what you are talking about. I gave him the pendent back. I do not have it," she murmured feebly.

"Yes you do! You lie!" She threw her back against the wall. Pain scaled her body with every breath she took. "The pendent can never be put back together. I cursed it after your mother broke it."

"Then I do not know what to tell you. He will forget about me…"

"He never forgets that is the problem! You are the only thing that stands in my way." A long sliver dagger appeared in Esmeralda's hand. "And I am going to get rid of you."

"Leave her alone!" her father cried weakly, but his pleas went unnoticed.

She lunged at Lucy. Lucy rolled out of the way but not in time, Esmeralda grabbed her long hair. "I will make this short and sweet." She brought the dagger to Lucy's throat. She could feel the cold blade touch her skin. "It will be sweet for me, and hopefully, painful for you."

Her fingers searched the wooden floor for the small letter opener that she had stumbled across earlier. Finally, her fingers found it. She used it to protect her from the blade of the dagger.

"You think that is going to stop me! Ha! Foolish girl you can not kill me." She kicked Lucy to the ground.

"Stop Esmeralda!" A cold deep voice came from the corner of the attic. "Kill her and I will kill you."

"Jaire you know no living being can do that. So quite stalling and say good bye to her now." Her fingers gasped Lucy's long hair as she brought the dagger to her throat again.

"I am sorry Jaire." Lucy whispered. "I never meant to hurt you, I really do love you." Tears slipped down her pale cheeks like the rain falling from the dark clouds.

"I know no human can kill you but," Jaire casually walked by Esmeralda, "a spirit can. I know one that you caused so much pain and she is just aching for some of that sweet stuff you talk so much about. You hurt her so bad she just came to get revenge." A white figure floated up the stairs. The light was blinding.

"Mother?" Lucy cried weakly.

"Lilliana," her father mumbled his limbs felt weak and his vision was blurred.

"Esmeralda you have cause so much pain for one vessel. Now it is time to end your reign of suffering." Lilliana took the letter opener from Lucy's hand. Her fingers were warm and her eyes were stern as she approached Esmeralda.

Lilliana drove the weapon into Esmeralda's chest. Esmeralda cried as black blood oozed from her chest. Her eyes dimmed and her skin turned ashen. Her body erupted into a ball of flames. Lucy was thrown against the wall. The only thing left of Esmeralda was her dark ashes.

Lilliana stood in the center of the room her long white robe shone in the light. "Lilliana, please forgive me for what I did to you." Christopher pleaded.

"Christopher there is no need to apologize look at what you have done. You have raised two wonderful children who will become resourceful adults. Love is forever and I will always love you." She touched his hand and kissed his lips. Tears ran down his cheeks and she whisked them away with a flick of her ghostly hand. "There will be no more I am sorry's, there has been too many of them."

She turned to Jaire. "Lilliana, I am sorry for breaking your heart and there is not a moment in the day that I do not remember the look on your face and the tears in your eyes." Tears broke free from his eyes. He could barely breathe as he stared into her beautiful eyes.

"In life I loved you and in death I will, but you need to take care of my daughter because she needs you. Our love was the past and hers is the present." She kissed away his tears.

"Johnathan," she called. He walked up the stairs. His eyes were red and tears escaped from his eyes. "Your family will always be there for you. I am always with you no matter how old you get. In your memory I will be preserved forever, but you must not dwell in the past for your future is in the present." She hugged Johnathan tightly.

"Johnathan no matter what you must never summon me. Sweet heart there are many obstacles in your life and there will be more to come. My dear Johnny you must never call me no matter what happens. Please promise me this." Johnathan nodded wordlessly.

"And for Lucy I have this." She handed Jaire an envelope. She stooped beside her daughter and ran her fingers through her long dark hair. Lilliana wept. "For you my dark angel I have the world to give you, but I will have to wait for death, because life is the only boundary for us, my dear. The heavens are the limit for you my little dark angel." She kissed Lucy's hair as tears fell from her eyes. "I will always be with you, forever and always my dear little dark angel." Lilliana slowly walked to the window and faded back into the night.

Part Two

Chapter Nine
"Love Isn't Always Enough"

Her eyes fluttered open. She rubbed her head; it was wrapped in a bandage. "What happened?" She looked around flowers and cards and large stuffed animals surrounded her. A boy with long blonde hair was asleep in a chair next to her bed.

She tapped his shoulder. "Hello?" He jerked up and smiled.

"Lucy you are finally awake. Wait here I will get your brother and father. They can not wait to see you." He rushed out of the room. When he came back a boy and a man followed him.

"Oh Lucky you are finally awake." The man rushed to wrap his arms around her; her body stiffened and tensed.

"Hey Luce what is the matter?" The boy asked softly.

"Who are you? Why do you keep calling me Lucy?" she questioned. She frowned in confusion.

"Oh no." The blonde haired boy moaned. "This is what I was afraid of she has lost her memory. This is all Esmeralda's doing. Johnathan call the doctor in," he cried.

"Who is Esmeralda? Will someone please tell me what is going on?" she demanded.

"Lucy I am your father, Christopher Montgomery," He pointed to the boy next to him, "This is your twin brother Johnathan Montgomery and he is Jaire DeCrothro he is a very good friend of yours. You are in a hospital you had a very bad accident."

"Which I will explain to you later." The boy named Jaire said softly. "I can not believe this. I knew she would do something like this."

"Mr. Montgomery, oh Lucy you are awake." A man in a white coat walked in smiling.

"Do I know you?" she asked curiously.

"My name is Dr. Jones, I use to take care of your mother when she was sick and you had your check-up about a day after you moved here," he said with a caring smile.

"Where is my mother?" she whispered.

"Lucy she died last year in a car accident. You do not remember anything?" Johnathan asked.

"I do not think so."

"This is typical Mr. Montgomery after a coma. I will do some tests and we will see the damage. Everything will be fine." Dr. Jones shook her father's hand then he walked out of the room.

"My mother died?" She covered her mouth.

"Yes, she did Lucky. Once they do the tests we will go back home and you will regain your memory." Her father held her close.

"How long was I in a coma?" she cried.

"Two months." Jaire whispered. She stared into his eyes there was something warm and familiar about them. She liked him.

"I can not wait to get out of here. I have only been awake a few minutes and I already have a headache." She laughed weakly.

"Come Mr. Montgomery she needs her rest she has a MRI tomorrow and the doctor would like her to be rested." A thin sweet nurse led her father and brother out of the room.

"Bye Lucky I will see you tomorrow." He kissed the top of her head.

"Yeah, Luce I will be here." Her brother hugged her lightly. Jaire waited until they left when he approached her.

"I will be here don't you worry. I will always be here for you." He kissed her cheek and hugged her close. "I will always be here for you. You saved me and now it is my turn to save you," he whispered softly into her ear as he released her from a gentle hug.

"Mr. DeCrothro it is time to leave Miss Montgomery and let her get some rest." The nurse said sternly. "Good night sweet heart."

"Good night." She walked around the room. The scent of flowers clung to the air and cards littered the tables. She picked up one and it was sealed so she tore it open. When she opened it a broken pendent fell out she read the card.

Until we are together this will be yours. You have my heart Lucy and we will put it back together once we are together again. You saved me. You gave me a reason to change who I use to be; you are my reason for living.
Forever yours,
Jaire DeCrothro

"Boy, we must have been close. I feel like I have known you my whole life." She put the pendent on. The jewel glowed happily. She crawled in bed. She smiled in her sleep. "Jaire," she whispered as she entered her dreamland.

"What am I suppose to do Jaire? My little girl doesn't even know who I am," Lucy's father cried.

"She does. It is at the back of her mind. She knows who we are I can feel it when she looks at me and eventually she will remember us. But for now it is better that she does not," Jaire whispered as he drank his coffee, he winced at its bitterness.

"What is that suppose to mean?" he demanded.

"What I mean is that there is so much pain in that girl's mind. She has no idea how to deal with it. We will tell her little by little. We started off with Lilliana's death. I could see memories flicker in her mind, but we do not want to drive her away. Listen to me Christopher I can feel her pain. Between life and death is a dark place to be. "

"I guess you are right I just want my little girl to be back to normal. I love her so much. Her and Johnathan are all I have of Lilliana and I do not want to lose either one of them. They are the world; the air I breathe and I need them."

"I love your daughter very much and I will try everything in my power to get her back to us. She saved my life her, and Lilliana, and I am not about to lose her." Jaire stood up.

"Where are you going?" he asked softly.

"Going home." Jaire answered coolly as he started to leave.

"Not this late, you will stay in the spare bedroom it is right down the hall from Lucy's room. There should be everything you need." Chris nodded. "Oh by the way, thank you for saving my life and Lucy's." Jaire nodded as he headed for his room.

Jaire could hear the sound of a screaming guitar and thundering drums. He knocked softly. He could hear Johnathan turn down the stereo and whisper, "Come in."

"Hello Johnathan. What are you doing?" He stared at the computer screen and saw the topic, *Amnesia victims and how they regained their memory.*

"Do you think this is going to help her?" Jaire asked.

"I do not know, but it is worth a try." Johnathan turned off the computer.

"She needs her family more than medication. Love is the only remedy."

"Sometimes love isn't enough. If it was then how come she is in the state she is in now?" Johnathan cried.

"If it weren't for your love for her or my love she would have been killed!" Jaire argued.

"Yes, but if she hadn't loved father she would have never been hurt in the first place. She cares to damn much!" Johnathan slammed his fist down on the table shaking its contents.

"She loves her family she would have died for you and your father. She does care, but you should not condemn her for it you should lover her even more. Life throws us curves and we must get past it. It is the changes that can make or break you. Do not let them destroy you like I let them destroy me." Jaire rose. "Good night Johnathan." Jaire left the room.

Chapter Ten

Homecoming

When the mini van pulled in Jaire and Johnathan were waiting impatiently. They had been waiting for this moment since she woke up. They were finally going to be together once again. The doctor had told them the damage to her brain was very small and she should gain her memory with time.

"Hello we are home!" Chris called.

"Oh, this is so beautiful. It is so large," she said in awe.

"That is what you said the first time that you saw this place. Your room is across from your brother's. Upstairs."

"Thank you daddy," she whispered. She touched his arm lightly, unsure of what to do next. She walked up the handsome staircase; her fingers glided over the shiny wood. She imagined a large band playing in the corner and her father and brother dressed in tuxes, but as fast as it came it disappeared.

"What is the matter Lucy?" her father called to her.

"Nothing." She continued up the stairs; she felt like she was lost in a daze. Everything seemed so new, and yet, so familiar, she remembered shards and tidbits of her past. When she walked into her room she was caught by surprise by the pink walls and carpet.

"You hated pink." Johnathan walked into the room.

"Then what is up with the walls and carpet?" she asked as she stared at the posters and books that lined her wall.

"This was mother's room when she was our age and mother loved the color pink. I am right across the hall if you need me Luce." He smiled comfortingly.

"Thank you Johnathan." He waved good bye as he walked out of her room. She searched through her books for something but she did not know what. She scanned the photo albums but all she could remember was vague images.

She stared at a picture of her and her brother standing next to a moving van. She was smiling, but Johnathan stared defiantly at the camera. "Who are you?" she asked herself as she looked into the mirror. She touched the pendent delicately. Her mind felt light every time she fingered it as if there was some strange power that laid waiting for her to release it.

That night after everyone fell asleep Lucy laid awake staring at the ceiling questioning her existence. Pictures and books were scattered on her bed and floor. Her memories were hiding from her as if she was just apart of their silly game. She closed her eyes and drifted into a restless sleep.

She was walking up narrow steps; Johnathan followed closely behind. She could hear the sound of a woman laughing cruelly. She saw her father tied to a chair. He was yelling at the woman. She watched the woman slap her father. She called to him, but she felt Johnathan's hand covered her mouth.

He whispered for her to leave. She shook her head and crept up the stairs into the room. She was behind her father untying the ropes that held him to the chair when she felt a searing pain in her head. The woman held Lucy by the hair when she looked up into the eyes of the woman her body froze they were like green flames.

Lucy woke up screaming. Jaire nearly ripped the door from the wall as he headed into her room. He flew to her side and wrapped his arms around her. "Shhh! It is all right." She breathed heavily into his chest her tears stained the front of his white tee shirt. His arms felt warm and welcoming as if she had been in this situation before.

"Lucy what is the matter?" her father panted. His robe was untied and his feet were bare. His dark hair was pushed over one side and his eyes were bloodshot from the lack of sleep.

"It is nothing Daddy. It was just a bad dream." She could feel Jaire tighten his hold on her slightly.

"Oh, that is it." He breathed a sigh of relief. "Good night Lucky." He kissed the top of her head before he staggered out of the room.

"What was the dream about?" Jaire whispered softly as she snuggled closely.

"Johnathan and I were going up a narrow staircase and then we were in a dark room. Daddy was tied to a chair and arguing with a woman. I went to untie the ropes but the woman caught me and all I remember was her green eyes they made my body turn icy. It seemed so real." She shook. Jaire's body tensed. "What's the matter? Why are you so tense?"

He snapped out of his clouded thoughts. "No reason. Good night Lucy." He got up to leave but she grabbed his arm.

"Will you please stay with me, at least until I fall asleep?" she asked softly, the dream was still fresh in her mind. She shivered, but nothing seemed to shake away the cold that surrounded her.

"Yes, I will." He held her close. It was not long before she fell asleep. Her mind and body was tired. Jaire hated leaving her. He stared at her; he pushed her dark hair from her face and smiled.

"Love finds us, Lucy, we do not go looking for it. You are my life, my love." He kissed her eyes. He pulled the blanket over her arms. Her arm was scarred. He could still hear her words that night echoing throughout the walls of his mind.

Lilliana haunted his dreams at night, she told him how Lucy would recover her memory but as the sun rises each morning he forgets her words. He kissed Lucy once more before he left her room.

He walked around the grounds. Visions of him and Lilliana flooded his mind. He could hear her laughter by the old oak on his right; he could still feel her hand in his as he walked to the hidden gazebo. Jaire traced the heart on the beam of the gazebo. He had loved her and she had loved him nothing in the world could change how he felt or what he did.

Chapter Eleven
"Nothing is ever forgotten"

When Lucy walked out of her room the next morning she found the house empty. Fear made her panic. She called for her family but no one answered her call. She looked on the refrigerator and spotted a small note.

Sorry Lucy I have a meeting to attend and Johnathan's at lessons. Jaire should be over. I love you.
Daddy

She stared around the kitchen and she felt as if she was the only person on the face of the earth. She wandered around the house, not focusing on anything until she spots a cord hanging from the ceiling. She wraps her fingers around it.

"Lucy don't!" Jaire cried. He pulled her away from the cord. "You are not ready to go up there just yet. Believe me." His dark green eyes pleaded with her. She gazed at him.

"I understand. When will I be able to go up there?" she asked curiously.

He kisses her forehead. "You will know it. Come let's go for a walk down to the creek. I have a basket waiting in the refrigerator waiting for us." He led her by the hand down stairs.

"Jaire why don't you want me to up there? It is just an attic." She shrugged as she held onto the basket. "I might remember something while I am up there."

"There are memories that you do not want to remember, believe me." He smiled casually. She thought she saw sadness and anger flicker in hi eyes, but she just shrugged it off. "Concentrate on one memory at a time. The good ones would be the best before you remember the more painful ones."

"I just want to know," she begged.

"I know and you will know in time. We are here." He pointed to the small babbling creek.

"Oh it is beautiful. Look there is a little cottage over there," she said in awe.

"That is my cottage," he whispered.

"Why don't we have our lunch there?"

"It is very beautiful, the sun is shining and the birds are chirping. I think it is nice outside." He laid back against the tree.

"You are right. It is very beautiful. You know that since I have come home it seems as if the sun has been shining more than it did before." She laid next to him the grass. She picked a small purple flower and rubbed its velvet petals.

"What do you mean?" Jaire asked sleepily.

"I remember it raining all of the time. I remember sitting out in the rain under a tree, but that is all. I just remember the rain." She laid back. "But now it seems almost impossible for the rain to come."

"It will come along with..." Jaire closed his eyes. He fell asleep. She smiled to herself.

He is beautiful. His long blonde hair was tied back behind his head and his pale skin was starting to tan. She touched his hand and it was warm; something inside of her made her smile.

She walked to the cottage but stopped when she saw the gazebo on the hill. She felt drawn to it. Once she stepped inside of the gazebo she felt dizzy. Images flashed before her eyes. She saw Jaire's back in the dark and then a little black book in her hands. "What does this all mean!?" she cried. "What does this have to do with me?!" She kicked the side of it. She could hear voices in her mind. She could hear her brother's and her father's. Tears fell from her dark eyes as she tried to make sense of what was happening to her.

Raindrops fell on Jaire's face. He awoke with a start. *Rain? Oh no!* He ran toward the cottage. He opened the door. "Lucy! Where are you?" he yelled through the house. "Where are you?"

He stopped when he heard someone screaming in the distance. "What does this all have to do with me?!" *It is Lucy!*

He rushed outside and found her crying in the center of the alcove on the hill. Her hair was plastered against her face and her face was stained from crying. He hurried toward her and embraced her. She buried herself in his chest and cried. The rain held them inside the gazebo but Lucy was trapped inside her own mind.

"I just do not get it!" she cried. "I see all these things and hear all these voices inside my head, but I can not put them together. What am I doing wrong!?" she panted.

"You are doing nothing wrong." He stroked her hair. Her body trembled beneath his. He pulled her face away from his shirt but she turned away. "Look at me Lucy. You are doing nothing wrong. Just give it time." He kissed her lips.

"I know I have to give it time, but when I look into my father's eyes I know he expects me to get my memory back right then. I can feel he is holding something back. I just know it; you all are and I will figure it out."

He kissed the top of her head. "I have no doubt in my mind that you will." The sun started to poke through the clouds. "Looks like we better get you home before your dad worries."

"He said he wouldn't be back until later, why can't we stay just a little longer? It is so nice here. The mountains are so beautiful and the creek is lovely." She snuggled closer to Jaire as they walked to the cottage.

"Okay," he whispered.

"Jaire?" she asked.

"Yes, what is it Lucy?" he asked softly as he stared out the window. The sun had pushed away the dark clouds and was now shining happily in its sky.

"How did we meet? Where did we meet?" she asked curiously as she sat up to look at him.

"Well," He paused for a moment. "We met while you were riding your bike. You were not paying attention to what you were doing and you almost crashed into that tree over there." He pointed to a large pine tree. "But I stopped you and your bike, you had passed out before I saved you. So I brought you in here and stayed until you woke up but then you passed out again and your father came and got you. And the rest is history."

"But how did we become friends if I only saw you once?" Lucy asked.

"The next day you came back to return my blanket that I had given you to keep warm, but I wasn't home so you left it and then you spotted that little gazebo on the hill and…"

"And I sat there reading a little black book." She could feel the book in her hands for some time.

"Yes. Then it started to rain and when you were about to leave when you passed out again and I took you inside. Do you remember anything about the book you were reading?" Jaire asked eagerly.

"No, all I remember is that it was black and there was a note inside of it. But that is it, it is as if my mind is blocking it out. I can not get passed it." She walked toward the window. "I think we should get home now. I do not want daddy to worry or Johnathan."

"Yes, we should get home and Lucy," He turned her toward him, "there will be more rain, but I hope the sun will shine more in your life than it did before." He kissed her hand as he guided her out of the house. *Things will be different this time Lucy I can promise you that.*

Chapter Twelve
Bad Dreams

The next few weeks flew by like a dream in Lucy's mind. She only could remember little bits. Her brother and his first solo in the band, her father's Mother's day present for her mom, and her mother staring at the mirror while she was getting ready for a party, but nothing after she moved to Kentucky. Her past still remained a mystery to her.

Everyday her and Jaire would rake leaves outside or go for long walks around the grounds. When the first snow fell they made snowmen and snow angels. "I wish this would never end." Lucy cried as she fell back into the snow.

"I know. It is almost heavenly," he breathed. She snuggled close to him.

"Look over there! It is a little hideaway over there in the trees. Come on lets go!" She ran toward it. Her heart pounding in her chest. The cold wind blew through her long hair.

Jaire was racing behind her. His long legs made him travel faster until he was right behind her. "Ah!" she cried as she felt his hand on her hips. They tumbled in the snow until they were at the foot of the old gazebo.

"Oh Jaire it is lovely. I wonder how long it has been here." She circled in the middle. Her eyes scanned every piece of wood.

"Before you were born." His fingers glided along the cool wood.

"Jaire what this?" She pointed to the heart.

"Let me see." He gasped. He had almost forgot where that was.

"*JD + LW*. What does that mean Jaire?" she asked as she traced the heart with her index finger.

"LW is your mother. Lilliana Ward…"

"But I thought mother's name was Lilliana Rojas?" she queried. Her finger stopped on JD. "Who is JD then?"

"Lucy it is getting dark I think we should get back inside. It is very cold." His lips were turning blue and his face was losing its color.

"Jaire are you all right?" She ran to his side before he fell to the ground.

"I just have to get inside; it is very cold out here Lucy." He walked out of the gazebo with Lucy by his side.

"Jaire what's the matter?" Her father asked when they walked through the door. Jaire pulled out a chair and sat down. His body trembled from the memories that had flooded his mind. He could not hold onto his sanity.

"Just my past," he muttered when Lucy went to make him a cup of hot tea. "I found the gazebo where Lilliana and I use to have our picnics in and such after Lucy had come home, but today we found it and I guess I just lost it." He took a deep breath. "She is lucky she can not remember what happened."

Her father slammed his fist down on the table and whispered angrily, "do not ever say that. She has to get her memory back!"

The sound of something breaking echoed throughout the kitchen. "Lucy!" Jaire ran to Lucy. He found her standing next to a broken pink teacup. Her face was white as snow and tears brimmed her eyelashes. Her breathing was ragged and her hands trembled.

Drops of blood ran down her wrist. "Daddy," she cried. "I am sorry. I must have dropped it." She bent down to pick one of the shards of porcelain from the ground but she dropped it and cut her hand again.

"Lucy stop!" Jaire grabbed her arm. Blood covered his hand. "Come with me."

She nodded silently. He took to the bathroom where the first aid kit was kept.

"What is the matter Lucy? What happened?" He rubbed a cotton ball over her palm.

"I remembered something and it scared me." Her voice quivered.

"What was it?"

"A pair of cold green eyes and a little pink teacup shattering across the floor." She sighed. "It had to be just my imagination. Those eyes could not have belonged to anyone, they made my body go cold and stiff." She looked down at her hand. "Thank you Jaire. You are really kind." She kissed his lips.

"I better go to bed. It is very late." She stood up and smiled weakly.

"I better go home before it gets to late," Jaire whispered.

"Why don't you stay here for the night? It is severely chilly and I do not want anything to happen to you." She took his hand and led him to the room down from hers. He could not take his eyes off of her. Her dark hair fell softly on her shoulders and her dark blue eyes were full of mystery; he turned to her and stared into her deep eyes. He brought his lips down to hers and kissed her tenderly.

"Lucy…" he whispered as he stepped back.

"Jaire what is it?" she asked breathlessly.

"It is late and you need your rest." He rested his forehead against hers. He kissed her quickly on the cheek and retreated to his room.

Lucy felt as if she was lighter than air. Once she was in her room she fell back into her bed and sighed happily. She felt like there was a hundred butterflies fluttering around in her stomach. Her eyes grew heavy as she began to fall asleep.

She was once again creeping up the steps with her brother trailing behind her. She could see her father tied to a chair and a woman with fiery red hair standing over him. Her voice was thick and menacing. Her father yelled at the woman. She winced when she saw the woman hit her father. Blood oozed from his nose.

She cried out to him. Her brother covered her mouth, but she pushed him away. When she was behind her father she could hear him begging her to leave him be but she told him no. Then the woman pulled her up from the ground by her hair; the woman laughed when she yelled at her. The next thing she knew the back of her head was hurting. She tried to touch it, but she was tied to a chair.

She struggled, but the ropes just cut deeper and deeper into her skin. She could feel the warmth of her blood flowing from her veins down her hands. The woman's words were vague and her pain was immense, but she stared at her father who continued to scream and threaten the woman with red hair. The woman hit her father one more time and blood poured from his skull.

"No!!" she cried. Sweat poured from her forehead and her sheets were soaked. Her heart raced in her chest. She could barely breathe. Her body ached. She stared at her wrists. Scars covered them. Her hands shook.

Jaire rushed into her room. "Lucy what's the matter?" he cried. She held out her scarred wrists.

"Jaire where did I get these?" she whispered softly.

"Lucy…" He cried gently.

"Where in the hell did I get these scars!? Tell me Jaire! I am tired of being put off," she cried. He shook his head with sorrow.

"I can't. I made a promise." He walked toward her and pulled her to him. She pushed him away. "Who did you make the promise to? Daddy?"

"No," He took a deep breath. "Your mother."

"But she is dead!" She pushed him to the ground. "I am tired of being lied to! My mother is dead! How could you possibly know her?"

"I knew her when she was your age." Involuntarily she reached for the pendent. He walked toward her.

"How could you? She is older than you are." She grasped the pendent tighter; the edges cut into her skin, but she did not release it.

"I did know her," he whispered. "She is not older than I am; I knew her and your grandmother a long time ago," he whispered.

"How can that be!" she cried. The pendent burned beneath her palm.

"I am sorry you have to…I just can not tell you now the pain is still there. All I can tell you is that you must find your mother's diary. Some of your questions will be answered. I am sorry that I can not be more helpful but…"

"Your promise to my mother?" she said skeptically. "Do you know where my mother's diary is?" she whispered.

"Only you had it," he whispered. He touched her hand lightly. "Lucy you must know this, I would die for you so you would never feel an ounce of pain." He kissed her hand and walked out of the room.

Her hands shook as she lay back in bed. She could not fall asleep nor did she want to. *What is happening to me?* She thought as she walked around the room. She stared out the window as rain pelted the house.

On her desk was a picture of her and her mother. She cradled it in her arms. "Mom how could have you known Jaire when you were sixteen? What is your secret?" she cried but her mother continued to smile at her.

Chapter Thirteen
Found

Days have gone by and the only thing Lucy found was a headache. She avoided her father and Jaire; the only one who seemed to understand her was her brother. He would listen to her and nod when he needed to but he never said a word.

"Johnathan what am I going to do? I feel, as if I am going to go out of my mind, am I crazy?" she cried as she fell back into his bed.

"Luce you are not crazy do not ever say that, you are just going through a tough time and it will pass like the others." His smoky eyes darken.

"What are you hiding from me? There is something that is haunting all of you, but you will not tell me. Why won't you?"

"It is complicated, Luce, but you will know in time." He sighed. "Tell me about the dream you are having."

"Johnathan it is horrible! We are going up some kind of stairs and then I see daddy tied to a chair and a woman with red hair is yelling at him. He keeps on yelling at her; you tell me something then I see the woman hit daddy. I try to cry out, but you cover my mouth then I push you away and as soon as I am able to untie daddy she grabs me by my hair. You are gone when I look back at the steps and then she hits me again and that's all I remember." She took a deep breath.

"Johnathan are you all right?" His face paled and he began to tremble.

"I am so sorry Luce. I had to…" His voice trailed off. Tears formed at the corner of his eyes. He balled his hands into fists and grimaced in pain. "I am so sorry. I had to…" He wrapped his arms around her and cried into her shoulder.

"Johnathan what is the matter? What are you sad about it was just a dream?" She ran her fingers through his brown hair.

"Yeah, a very bad dream. I have the same dream both morning and night; I can not forget it. Luce, you know I love you and so do dad and Jaire. I tried to protect you and to stop you but…"

"That wasn't just a dream was it Johnathan?" He turned away. "Johnathan answer me! Please I can not bear the silence from you," she begged.

"Luce we love you I can not tell you. I am sorry." He held her close but she pushed him away.

"Why is everyone treating me like I am five!? I can handle my past!" He grabbed her by the hand. "I can handle the pain. I already feel it lurking in the back of my mind. I need to know Johnathan."

"I can not help you." She ran out of the room and into hers. She gathered her backpack and shimmied out the window.

"I can not take this anymore." Once she hit the ground she ran full speed down the road. Her memory danced in front of her, luring her with false hopes and promises. The snow around her glistened with ice as rain came pouring out of the sky.

"Why me?" She ran to the gazebo on the hill. She fell in the center she crossed her arms and legs and prayed to God to make everything go away. "Let it wash away with the rain. Please." Tears streaked her face.

She laid against her backpack. She could not figure out why she brought it. She rummaged through it. She pulled out sheets of paper, random articles of clothing, and a small black book. She opened it. The pages were empty. She turned every page, but there were no words. Everything was blank as her mind.

"Why can't anything go right for once? Why does life have to be so cruel and unfair? Why does it have to take away the most important things in our life? In my life?" she screamed at the sky only the sound of thunder in the distance.

"To make us stronger. Loss is something that everyone deals with and it

is what you do that makes you who you are. It can make or break you." A voice in the back of her mind answered.

She buried her head in her hands. She could feel a warm tingly feeling run down her spine. Her vision blurred and she felt dizzy. Lucy stood up and tried to walk out of the gazebo, but she fell to her knees.

Drops of a silvery liquid fell from the sky and in a small puddle at the foot of the gazebo. Her eyes fluttered open painfully. A woman wearing a glimmering white robe stood in front of her. Lucy's heart froze and all of her tears melted away.

"Lucy." The woman whispered. Her long auburn cascaded down her shoulders and her gray eyes smiled. "My dear, you have grown into a beautiful young woman." She took a seat on the bench.

"Who are you?" she asked softly.

"Come and take a seat next to me and I will answer all of your questions to the best of my abilities." She ran her fingers through Lucy's dark hair.

"Who are you?" Lucy repeated.

"My dark angel," she whispered as she sighed softly. "Do you know who you are?"

"Yes…no, not really. Everything is changing and I can not keep up. Jaire will not tell me anything and neither will my brother or father. They say it is too painful. Do you know what happened the night of my accident?" she cried.

"Yes I do Lucy. But you need to remember by yourself; all I can do is help you along a little." She picked up the little black book and opened it.

"I think that is my mother's diary but the pages are blank." Lucy touched the cover of the book.

"Is it?" She turned it toward Lucy and her mother's handwriting appeared on the page. "There are things in here that will help you remember and things you will want to forget. But do not let the pain overwhelm you. Jaire has something for you and will give you it later." She kissed Lucy on the cheek.

"When will that be?" Lucy asked.

"The time will present itself." Tears streaked her cheeks as she wrapped her arms around Lucy. "Lucy, my little dark angel, I will always love you. I want you to take care of your brother and father they need you just as much as you need them." She kissed Lucy on the forehead. "Jaire will need you now. I will always love *all* of you."

"Mother…" She realized. "Mom don't go! I need you!" Lucy ran after her mother.

"Lucy, I will always love you. My little dark angel…" Her voice drifted into the wind's endless sea.

"No don't leave me again mommy! Please don't," she cried as her eyes fluttered open. She sobbed as she laid across the gazebo. "Don't go, I need…"

Chapter Fourteen
Truth Be Told

"Lucy!" Jaire rushed to the alcove. Lucy was lying on her side in the center of the gazebo. "Are you all right?" He scooped her in his arms and held onto her. Her eyes slowly opened.

"Jaire?" she whispered feebly.

"Yes?" he whispered back. A feeling of relief exploded in his chest.

"I saw my mother." Tears lined her eyelids. Jaire took a deep breath as he drew her closer to his chest. "Mother said she loved you and always would. Jaire…"

He turned away but tears were along ways away, somewhere near his toes, but he could still feel her touch and hear her words. "Lucy you need to go home." He stood up and brushed his pants off.

She stood up and started to walk out of the gazebo when she turned, "You really did love her." She walked out and into the rain.

"Yes I did, Lucy. But I love you now and I will never leave you side," he whispered ethereally. His heart was heavy with sorrow and yet it was as light as a feather as he walked her home.

Lucy was walking up the steps to her bedroom when she turned and spotted a rope hanging from the ceiling at the end of the hall. She stared at it; the pendent burned her skin but she continued to walk toward it.

She felt her fingers grasp the thing rope. It felt soft and delicate against her skin.

She tugged it softly and part of the ceiling fell with it. A narrow flight of stairs fell with ceiling. She cautiously pressed her foot on the first step testing the strength of the wood. Once she was sure it was stable she gradually stepped up the stairs.

It was dark when she finally reached the top of the staircase. She ran her hands down the wall searching for a light. Once her fingers glided over a small metal plate she flicked the switch. The light flickered slowly on. She covered her mouth when she saw what it was.

Blood covered the flood; two chairs were thrown against the wall. Shards of rope were scatter across the floor and a pile of ashes was near the boarded window. She rested her back against the wall.

"You foolish girl no human can kill me." Lucy could see the woman's face. It was wild and evil, but beautiful and sinister.

"Stop Esmeralda!" Jaire's words echoed in her mind. He stood at the top of the stairs and her heart felt as if it was going to explode with happiness.

"You can not kill me so stop stalling." Esmeralda, *that was her name*, laughed as she held the dagger to her throat.

"I am sorry I never meant to hurt you Jaire. I will always love you." She could hear her words echo off of the attic walls.

"I may not be able to but..." Jaire's words floated into her mind as she saw her mother walk up the stairs. Her long silver robe floated around her and her auburn hair hung softly on her shoulders. She could feel her mother's fingers take the letter opener from her hands and thrust it into Esmeralda's chest. Her body exploded and Lucy was thrown against the wall.

Lucy panted. Her body ached from the memory of her accident but it wasn't an accident it was almost murder. "Oh my gosh," she whispered as she stared at her wrists tiny drops of blood seeped through her skin. She could barely breath as she touched her wrist.

Lucy stood up feebly, her knees buckled as she held onto a chair for support. Her backpack laid beside her. "I can't believe what happened," she whispered as she covered her eyes.

"Believe it." She heard a soft voice whisper in her ear.

She looked up and Jaire was standing by the stairs. His long hair was drenched and his was full of sorrow, but his eyes leapt with silent happiness. Jaire's shirt was soaked and ripped. "Jaire I didn't know…"

He shook his head and whispered. "It has made me stronger."

"Jaire. I am so sorry…" she whispered as he headed toward her.

"Shhh…there will be no more I am sorry's there has already been too many of them in your lifetime."

He knelt beside her. "Your mother wanted you to have this." He handed her an envelope.

"This is what my mother was talking about." She carefully opened the envelope.

Dear Lucy,

By the time you read this you will know everything, my love for your father, Jaire, Johnathan and you. I love you all so much but I want you to live your life without pain. Do not let Jaire get away. He is a good man and he will be good to you. He will always help you if you need it. My dark angel do not get discouraged because I will be with you forever more. I give you my love and my blessing.

Lilliana Ward, your mother.

"I can not believe what you have done for me, Jaire you saved my life." She held onto his hand.

"No, your mother did." He sighed, "You saved mine and I will spend eternity trying to repay you."

She pulled him close and whispered. "Eternity is an awfully long time." She kissed his lips.

"I know," he whispered.

The pendent fell from Jaire's hand as the pendent broke loose from Lucy's neck and landed on the floor next to one another. The cracks began to fade, as the halves became whole.

Printed in the United States
62743LVS00006B/189